TIME TOGETHER

Me and Grandpa

BY MARIA CATHERINE

ILLUSTRATED BY PASCAL CAMPION

PICTURE WINDOW BOOKS

THIS BOOK BELONGS TO:

- -

Morning reading time

Whispery fish time

Game-winning goal time

Windy smile time

Fix-it time

Dreamy nap time

Birds and bugs time

Sizzle and serve time

Thoughtful game time

Surprise hug time

Make a wish time

Time Together is published by Picture Window Books
A Capstone Imprint
1710 Roe Crest Drive
North Mankato, Minnesota 56003
www.capstonepub.com

Library of Congress Cataloging-in-Publication data
is available on the Library of Congress website.
ISBN: 978-1-4795-5796-7 (paper over board)
ISBN: 978-1-4795-5798-1 (paperback)

Summary:
Snapshots of a grandpa and child enjoying every day moments
together. From taking a nap to reading the newspaper, these
small moments are the ones that create big memories.

Concepted by:
Kay Fraser and Christianne Jones

Designer:
K. Fraser

Photo Credit:
Shutterstock

Printed in China by Nordica.
0914/CA21401518
092014 008470NORDS15